THANKSGIVING FEAST

By Quinlan B. Lee

Illustrated by Jim Durk

Based on the Scholastic book series "Clifford The Big Red Dog" by Norman Bridwell

10 9 8 7 6 5 4 3 2   04 05 06 07 08

Designed by John Daly

Printed in the U.S.A.   First printing, October 2004

SCHOLASTIC INC.

New York   Toronto   London   Auckland   Sydney
Mexico City   New Delhi   Hong Kong   Buenos Aires

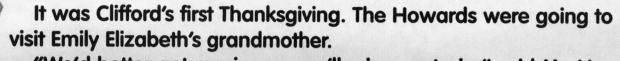

It was Clifford's first Thanksgiving. The Howards were going to visit Emily Elizabeth's grandmother.

"We'd better get moving, or we'll miss our train," said Mr. Howard. "It's really starting to snow out there."

"I'm almost ready, Dad," replied Emily Elizabeth. "I just have to find Clifford."

"And I just have to find my stuffing," added Mrs. Howard. "Where did I put it down?"

Mrs. Howard looked out the window. "You're right about the snow," she said. "We'd better bundle up. Here's your coat, Emily Elizabeth."

"And here's your stuffing!" said Emily Elizabeth with a laugh.

Mr. Howard laughed, too. "And here's Clifford!" he said.

At the train station, Mr. Howard hopped out of the taxi. "Hurry, everyone!" he called. "I'll get the luggage."

"Emily Elizabeth, I'll carry Daffodil," said Mrs. Howard. "You'd better carry Clifford. We wouldn't want to lose him in all this snow."

In the back of the taxi, Clifford barked.
"I almost forgot my stuffing!" cried Mrs. Howard. "Thank you, Clifford."
"Good job, boy," said Emily Elizabeth. She picked up Clifford and zipped him into her coat.

The Howards hurried across the station toward the ticket counter.
Emily Elizabeth spotted Nina, her parents, and Jorgé walking by. Clifford
barked happily and jumped out of Emily Elizabeth's arms to say hello.

"Nina!" called Emily Elizabeth. "What are you doing here?"

"We're on our way to a family reunion," said Nina. "We get together every Thanksgiving. Everyone brings a different dish and we all share stories."

"Hola!" said Nina's mother.
"My mom always brings her famous tamales," said Nina.
Jorgé licked his lips. He loved those tamales!

"I'd love to get your tamale recipe sometime," said Mrs. Howard.
"I'd be happy to share it with you," replied Nina's mother.
Mr. Howard looked at his watch. "But first we have to get our
tickets — we're running late!"

"You're in luck, folks," said the man at the ticket counter.
"These are the last three tickets on the eastbound train."

Clifford peeked out of Emily Elizabeth's jacket.
"Oh, excuse me," said the ticket man. "Do you need *four* tickets?"
Emily Elizabeth smiled. "Clifford and I will be sharing a seat."
"Sharing is what Thanksgiving's all about," replied the ticket man.

As Emily Elizabeth and her parents rushed toward their train, they heard a familiar voice calling to them. "Hello, Howard family!"
"Wait, Dad, it's Mr. Solomon!" cried Emily Elizabeth.

"Are you visiting family, too?" asked Mrs. Howard.

"I sure am," replied Mr. Solomon. "I'm going to see my sister, and Flo and Zo get to visit her turtles, Rico and Reena. This year I'm bringing my specialty—homemade cornbread!"

"It smells delicious," said Mr. Howard.

The Howards hurried onto the platform as the conductor called out, "All aboard!"

"That's our train," said Emily Elizabeth. "It looks like we made it just in time!"

The ticket man closed the train door. "Sorry, folks," he said. "You won't be getting on today."

"But you just sold us tickets," Mr. Howard said. "Remember? Three people and one small red puppy?"

"Oh, I remember," said the ticket man. "But no one's going anywhere today. The tracks are snowed under and won't be clear until morning."

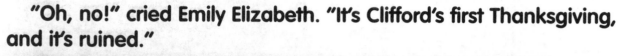

"Oh, no!" cried Emily Elizabeth. "It's Clifford's first Thanksgiving, and it's ruined."

"Don't worry, sweetheart," said Mrs. Howard. "We'll call Grandma and Grandpa and explain. We can still have a nice Thanksgiving at home."

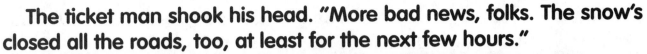

The ticket man shook his head. "More bad news, folks. The snow's closed all the roads, too, at least for the next few hours."

"So we can't get home, either?" Emily Elizabeth asked sadly.

"It's okay, honey," said Mr. Howard. "At least we're all here together."

The Howards settled down in the station cafeteria to wait out the storm.
"Room for one more?" asked Mr. Solomon.
Nina's family was close behind him. "How about three more and one hungry dog?"

"Of course, everyone," replied Mrs. Howard. "Here, I'm sure I can find some treats for some hungry animals." She reached into her bag and put some treats in front of Clifford and Jorgé. They pushed some over to share with Daffodil and Flo and Zo.

Seeing the animals share their treats gave Emily Elizabeth a great idea. "Hey, everyone," she said. "Let's share a Thanksgiving feast right here. We have stuffing, cornbread, tamales . . ."

"And a turkey!" added the ticket man.

Everyone looked at the ticket man with such surprise that he laughed. "I was supposed to take this turkey to a friend's house in the city when I got off of work, but the snow stopped that. There's plenty to go around."

"Come one, come all," said Mr. Howard. "This is what Thanksgiving is all about!"

"Emily Elizabeth, I know Clifford's first Thanksgiving didn't turn out like you hoped," said Mrs. Howard.

"It's even better!" said Emily Elizabeth. "Now Clifford will remember the true meaning of Thanksgiving — sharing with friends and family and being thankful for all you have."

Clifford barked, wagging his tail.

"You're welcome, Clifford," said Emily Elizabeth. "Happy Thanksgiving!"